SUN IN THE DARK

PREQUEL TO

BATTLEBORN SUNS MC

LEAH RHOADES

Copyright © 2022 by Dark Shifter Publishing
All rights reserved. This book or any portion
thereof
may not be reproduced or used in any manner
whatsoever
without the express written permission of the
publisher
except for the use of brief quotations in a book
review.

Printed in the United States of America

First Printing, 2022

Dark Shifter Publishing

KEEP UP WITH LEAH

https://www.facebook.com/Leah-Rhoades-Author-103448388138351

Other Titles by Leah Rhoades:

The Whisperer

Nightkind – Amore Immortale Vol. 1

Daywalker – Amore Immortale Vol. 2

Rogue

Crystal Rose

Chapter 1

A rustling breeze blew through crackling brown leaves outside the garage. But that provided little relief from the sweltering heat of an East Texas summer afternoon. Deacon swiped at his brow and his upper lip where beads of sweat gathered. He'd made a notable mess, but he'd seen far worse disasters changing motorcycle brakes.

Squinting against the sun, he checked his watch. Deacon Moore hadn't volunteered to work with the realtor the Battleborn Suns hired. But he had an appointment in an hour.

Grunting, he threw his tools in the box, half ass swiping oil stains with wads of paper towels. He had to shower and dress before getting across town.

As he dropped his gloves on the worktable, something small floated to the ground. A Polaroid, from one of those godforsaken photo booths. He clenched his teeth, staring at three genuine smiles that got him through rough times in Afghanistan. Now, they incited rage.

Brad and Tara didn't need to be at the forefront of his mind. Miserable fucks. He had business to handle. He crumpled the photo, dropping it in the trash and stomping into the house.

Home from his tour, grimy and exhausted, Deacon looked forward to coming home. Instead, he spent three days in hell, nowhere to go to wash away the sand and stink of the desert.

He scrubbed vigorously. He'd moved on. Still, the memory of his last shower with Tara had him showering in cold water. He didn't want to remember her curves or the way she'd smiled through her tears as they'd said goodbye.

Finished, he stepped out of the tub, toweling his skin with vengeance, as if to remove the darkness of his past. How had that fucking photo surfaced? He'd burned that shit long ago. A disturbing distraction when focused on, a task he didn't want!

He would never trust so blindly again. He reached into the closet for Dockers worthy of a business meeting, wishing a muscle shirt and torn jeans were appropriate. He had to represent a business.

Even if that business was owned by a bunch of ragtag ex-military bikers.

A Polo shirt and his silver chain around his neck followed, with riding boots. After all, he only had the bike.

He'd trimmed the short smattering of a chinstrap and thin line over his upper lip yesterday, so he skipped shaving and forewent the cologne. Gel finger-combed through his dark locks and he turned from the mirror, grabbing his keys and sunglasses.

The house was down the same County Road as Deacon's parents'. He took the long way, winding from the far end on the east side of town, just to avoid it. One reminder of betrayal a day was sufficient.

He turned onto the long driveway and assessed the property objectively. His crew didn't have much professional experience, but they worked hard and did a damn good job on the quaint little home, painted a welcoming blue.

He shut off the engine for a moment of quiet. He inhaled the scent of freshly cut grass, listened to the buzzing cicadas in the trees.

This wasn't their first work of art, transformed from a shack nearing collapse. But to turn real profit, expansion was crucial. A real estate agent had greater reach and knew the buying landscape.

The more they made, the more they could donate. The cause meant everything to Deacon. He'd returned to so much heartache. And he'd had nowhere to go. He couldn't stomach the thought of how many other vets suffered the same fate. He had a strong mind and still questioned his reason to live.

He never wanted another man – or woman – who risked their life for freedom and safety to face that hopelessness. Housing veterans who needed it most could mean saving lives.

☐

Chapter 2

Shiloh had a habit of arriving painfully early and had sat in her car for thirty minutes already. Her anxiety built as she thought about the heathens in the gangs back in Laredo.

She'd researched the Battleborn Suns before taking this appointment. Despite her misgivings, everything about their business seemed above board. And they all had military backgrounds. She wished she'd looked up Deacon Moore.

The distinct roar of a bike engine neared, and Shiloh watched the man on the machine pull into the dirt driveway a dozen yards away. She'd expected leather and a ponytail, but he had dressed respectfully. Special occasion or daily attire?

Either way, that ranked him above the cretins she'd known in her teens. When he finally dismounted, she rolled forward, parking beside him.

She hadn't expected this gorgeous, clean-cut specimen. But she couldn't flirt. This opportunity could launch her career. Her ambitions far outweighed any farfetched fantasy her deviant mind conjured.

She checked that her long, dark locks fell in place and pasted on a smile as he opened her car door, like a gentleman. He returned the grin, a dimple in his right cheek twitching. "Deacon Moore, I presume," she said.

"Yes, ma'am." His voice rang deep with a light drawl. "Please, call me Deacon."

He held out a hand, and she shook it, ignoring the tingle at his gentle but firm touch. "I'm Shiloh Quinn. It's great to meet you."

The pleasure's mine, ma'am."

Wasn't he the polite country boy? Shiloh would bet her boots he'd made women swoon. "Call me Shiloh." She motioned to the house. "It looks great. It set here unattended for nearly ten years. That's a lot of clean up."

He nodded, pride in his eyes. "It took some elbow grease. I hope you like what you see inside."

They'd trimmed trees and bushes, planted tulips in front. Shiloh guessed she'd find the interior impressive. "Lead the way."

Deacon started forward, climbing the steps to the whitewashed patio. He was distant but friendly, the kind of guy her mama would call 'raised right'.

9

He carried himself rigidly, confident, likely cultivated in the military. As he shoved the key in the lock, she noted he towered almost a foot over her, at least 6'2".

He opened the door, and Shiloh's boot heel clicked on pristine hardwood floors. Deacon flipped on the light, revealing subtle gray walls and a fan on the vaulted ceiling. The open floorplan showcased a huge kitchen island with granite counters and a farmhouse sink.

The dining room connected through an archway. She noted details like crown molding and decorative wall switches.

Shiloh followed the short hall, finding the bathroom. Dual vanity sinks, a walk-in shower, and a claw-foot tub with travertine tiles shone brilliantly in ample lighting.

She peered into the two bedrooms, carpeted in rich, short weave. The laundry room had a storage bench, table and sink. "You did a fantastic job. This will sell fast."

She gazed at Deacon. He turned away quickly, waving her past. He was polite, yet gave the impression he desperately wanted to get away from her. Did he have somewhere else to go, or some aversion to her?

Paranoia niggled at her as she strode back to the living room. "Do you think we'll get our price point?" He sounded almost irritated.

She gave Deacon her best winning smile. "I say list it for twenty more. You'll have a bidding war on your hands."

That smile she'd admired returned. "Really?"

"Oh, yeah. We'll have an open house Saturday. I'll stage some furniture so it feels like home."

He nodded. "You're the expert."

Shiloh had only gotten her real estate license a year ago but had an eye for what would sell. This was a masterpiece. "Great. I'll email you the details."

He hesitated, and Shiloh wanted to crawl under his skin, find what made him tick. Finally, Deacon said, "I'll be on my way. I appreciate your time."

So formal. Sighing internally, she shook his hand. "This'll be profitable for all of us." She pivoted and headed to the car. She watched him until he rounded the corner out of sight.

Deacon fit none of her preconceived notions of bikers. Hopefully, the other Battleborn Suns weren't so damn sexy or intriguing. Deacon had already weaseled under her skin.

Chapter 3

Deacon raced around the curves, distance vital. He didn't mind admiration, but Shiloh Quinn's interest ran deeper, if he knew anything about women.

Of course, running from them was arguably his best skill. So, maybe he didn't know much.

He clenched his jaw. He dreaded working with her. Sex appeal that strong challenged even his conviction. Long, shapely legs and obvious but gentle curves gave the illusion of height. Her dark hair framed an elegant face with full lips, and those crystal blue eyes sparked every time she glanced at him.

He revved the engine, speed his friend. He cursed the vibrating phone in his pocket, not wanting to stop until he reached a safe place to curb his desires. Grunting, he turned into the corner store parking lot and whipped out the phone, barking, "What?"

"Deacon, there's a situation at the Paris house," River Watson shouted over the din of construction.

Noah handled 'situations'. Why call him? "Call Noah."

"Bro, Noah is the situation," River clarified. "How far are you?"

Deacon was drained after facing bad memories and the all too feminine realtor. But the Suns gave him something to believe in, a family when everyone else bailed. He owed them. And a quick ride out would distract him. "Fifteen minutes. Maybe twenty."

"Make it twelve or we'll have fuzz," River warned, hanging up. Fuck. The cops hated that the Suns did nothing illegal and would happily intervene.

Deacon roared out, hitting the highway at top speed. He exited and leaned into the curves through the older neighborhood. No red and blue lights flashed as he pulled up to the curb amidst the other bikes.

He did, however, see Noah, nose to nose with some guy, chests puffed. As he cut the engine, the argument hit him at full volume. Deacon stepped between them, putting a flat hand to each chest.

"What the fuck is the problem?" He looked back and forth, noting Noah's red face.

Pointing at the other guy, Noah spat, "Ask Sparky about the inspection."

The other man growled. "Sparky, huh? Funny, dirtbag."

Deacon addressed River, standing close by. "Fill me in before I break their jaws to shut them up."

River gawked. Deacon stayed low key, rarely angry. But he'd reached emotional capacity today. A brawl made a good outlet. "This is the electrician. Supposedly licensed. But we failed inspection."

Noah scoffed. "Failed! Shit, the inspector said our ten grand probably bought hookers and blow. We've got wrong gauge wires, overloaded circuits, code violations. This jackass wants more money to fix it."

Ten grand, wasted. This would kill their scheduling. In the flipping business, time was money. Deacon glared at the electrician. "You fucked up."

His eyes widened. Maybe he smelled Deacon's dangerous mood. "The inspector busted your balls, I swear. I got this for three."

"Three grand?" Deacon laughed humorlessly. "You should refund what we already paid. We'll hire someone who knows their shit."

"Come on, man," the electrician whined.

Deacon scented fear, fed off it like a predator. "How fast? No cutting corners. No balls busted, including yours."

The electrician nearly hyperventilated. "I need materials. Time—"

Deacon cut him off. "One week. And a grand, if the job's done right. Otherwise, we'll find a way to bleed our money out of you." The Suns weren't violent, but it was implied. Too bad, beating the guy might relieve stress.

His shoulders drooped. "Alright." He backed away.

"Be here at sunrise. I'd hate to have to come find you," Deacon added. The man ran toward his van, tires squealing as he pulled away.

River chuckled. "Damn, Deacon, I think he pissed himself."

Deacon shrugged, not making eye contact. He felt haunted, violent, and didn't need anyone reading him. "I had to make a point." He glanced at Noah.

"You can't lose your cool, bro. What the hell got into you?"

Noah's chest still heaved, but his expression calmed. "I have a schedule. When something collapses like this, it means reconfiguring everything to meet deadlines." He smacked Deacon's chest. "And no double standards. What bee got in your bonnet?"

Waving dismissively, he muttered, "Women and old wounds can bring out the worst in anyone."

River moved closer "So, things with the realtor went really well? Or totally bombed?"

Deacon sent him a warning look. "The agent's listing the house." To River, he added, "Stick your nose in my business, you end up wetting your pants." He strode eagerly toward the bike. He needed solitude. Tomorrow, he'd function again, after he festered a bit in the sharp pain of regret.

Chapter 4

Shiloh was unusually nervous. Small town girls rarely got big contracts. Selling this property meant an exclusive contract with the Battleborn Suns. As business grew, they would march toward Dallas.

A big city, like she'd always dreamed.

She bit her lip, looking for anything out of place. But she'd done her due diligence. Everything was perfect.

She jumped as the door unlatched. The open house started in twenty minutes. When Deacon strode in, she didn't know whether to laugh or cry. This man rattled her.

"I wasn't expecting you," she said, watching him sweep his gaze over the space. "It looks cozy. Welcoming."

Shiloh's chest puffed with pride. She wouldn't analyze why his opinion meant so much "That's the idea."

He met her gaze. "The guys wanted me to come see how open houses work. I'll stay out of your way."

Business, not personal. Shiloh chided herself for hoping. She told him, "People come look at the house. I point out features, answer questions. I explain the charity. Hopefully, we get several offers."

"Get offers today?" His eyes focused somewhere over her head.

Confidently, she said, "I expect it. But wait to see if there's a higher bidder."

"Okay." He walked out the front door. Deacon had a chip on his shoulder, though she didn't know why. She sensed danger below the surface. It drew her in but served as a warning.

The sound of an engine approaching refocused her. She couldn't daydream about Deacon and make the sale.

***

Deacon took down the 'open house' sign while Shiloh locked up. A successful day, flown by. He gazed at her, eyes guarded. She wanted to rip the mask off, but business took precedence.

"FYI, you have three offers already and at least four more people promising bids before the end of the week."

He blinked at her. "Is that normal?"

A laugh bubbled out. "The market is hot, but I've never seen this before. If all your work is this quality, people will come in droves."

"We never cut corners on quality." He held out a hand, and she accepted. "I'll see you soon."

Shiloh deflated. "I'll call you with news."

He walked away but hesitated midstep, mixed emotions all over his face. "Do you have plans?"

Shiloh's throat seized. He'd just thrown her a curve ball. "No."

"I thought we could celebrate." He added, "Not a date. Just dinner, my treat."

Acknowledged or otherwise, chemistry flowed between them. Shiloh longed to explore it. "I'd like that."

She followed his troubled gaze, aimed at her car. "You're not dressed for the bike. You want to follow me to Luigi's?"

Shiloh cursed her penchant for dresses and heels. But taking separate vehicles pervaded the non-date theme, apparently. "Sure. I'll check my messages and be on my way." Date or not, an evening spent with Deacon thrilled her, but she needed to breathe.

He straddled the bike. "I'll wait." He smirked and folded his arms on his chest.

Was he flirting? Her stomach tightening was unrelated to her appetite for Italian food. "Such a gentleman," she quipped back. His smirk blossomed into a grin, sending a shiver down her spine.

Deacon drove with better etiquette than any biker back home. She questioned her prejudice against the stereotype, she realized as she pulled into a parking space.

Her car door opened, Deacon a foot away. "Do all the Battleborn Suns have your sense of chivalry?"

The muscle in his jaw twitched. Amusement or irritation? "Some of us know how to treat a lady."

She followed him to the front of the restaurant. "And the others?"

He held the door, looking away. "I love my brothers, but there's a reason bikers get reputations as womanizers. No one's perfect."

Shiloh had yet to uncover Deacon's flaws.

Once seated, he stared out the window in silence. Curiosity plagued her. "How did you find the club? You don't fit the biker profile."

He met her gaze, eyes haunted. "I came home from Afghanistan with nowhere to go." Her jaw dropped, and he snorted. "It happens all the time." Shiloh didn't respond. She simply waited, and it paid off.

"I toured fresh from boot camp. Proud parents, fiancé waiting. My best friend, Brad, drove me to base. I sent money to Tara. She bought us a house." His jaw clenched. "I come home after two years, Uber home, and find her and Brad shacked up." He shook his head. "She answered the door in a sheet. Brad was behind her, ass naked."

Shiloh was disgusted. "That's unforgiveable."

He shrugged. "A lesson in trust." Shiloh noted the tension in his shoulders. His half smile didn't reach his eyes. "The money was gone. Brad handed me a fifty for a motel. I threw it at him and went to my parents."

Bitterly he continued, "My parents somehow drank the Kool-Aid. They were patriots when I left, anti-government conspiracy theorists when I came back.

Dad lost his job of twenty years, and they called me a traitor. I couldn't even stay the night."

Appalled, Shiloh shook her head. "How could they blame you?"

He shrugged. "All I wanted was to make them proud, and even that failed." He leaned back hard in his chair. "I got a room, took a shower. I dug a phone number from my wallet I could barely read, someone I'd served with. Reid was with the Suns. They've been my family since."

Everyone he loved failed him, broke his trust. And the Suns were the antithesis to the bullshit back home.

"This business is so important," he emphasized. "No one should experience that. Every veteran needs a home, temporarily or permanently. We can offer that."

That was a sucker punch to the chest. "You're building houses to donate," she stated in awe.

"We're misfits. We need jobs. We all got fucked. Pardon my language. So, we get paid, and everything else goes into donation properties."

Shiloh sat in awe. "That's beautiful."

He closed off instantly. Reluctantly, she changed direction. "I've had experience with MCs. I wrongly assumed they were all the same."

He grunted. "Are all women the same? Do you all play mind games?" Shiloh winced but saw a hope. Despite his demons, Deacon just admitted all women were like his fiancé. He cleared his throat, looking sheepish as their food arrived.

Eventually, he asked, "What's your experience with other MCs?"

Shiloh rolled her eyes. "In Laredo, they're gangs more than clubs." She wrinkled her nose. "Nothing but trouble. I moved to get away and start a career."

"Seems like an odd place to land."

She laughed sarcastically. "It's as close to Dallas as I could afford." Hard to find on a map. More difficult for your demons to follow you.

"Fair enough."

She welcomed the small talk that followed. Chatter about local dives, weather, and the real estate market was less traumatic than revisiting her past.

Deacon paid the check, and she thanked him as they left. His barriers were down as he walked her to her car, and it enticed her. Didn't he feel that connection?

"I guess we'll speak soon," he said, opening her car door. "Be safe getting home."

He turned, headed to his bike, but Shiloh made a spontaneous decision. She curled her fingers around his bicep, pulled him around, and pressed her lips to his. Deacon stiffened, but his hands fell on her waist as his mouth softened. Her skin caught fire.

Deacon pulling away abruptly. His eyes clouded, dousing her flames, and he shut down. "I have to go," he said flatly, striding to the bike and revving it.

Shiloh got behind the wheel and slammed the door. She'd crossed a line. She could've killed the contract. Still, she'd almost had him. She might still get to show Deacon how a real woman treated a man.

Chapter 5

Deacon tossed and turned for hours, until the clock glowed an offensive 5:30. His thoughts revolved around one thing, his body aching with desire. He knew better than to act on libido. His jaw hurt from clenched teeth, and his groin ached with a rampant case of self-inflicted blue balls.

But he preferred it to the pain of betrayal.

He'd fucked up. But he refused to succumb to selfish desire again.

He scrubbed his face and took a leak. He skipped the shower, planning on physical labor and sweat. He donned old, worn jeans, a beater that sniffed clean, and his boots. With a black ball cap and his vest, he hit the highway to Paris. The wind filled his lungs. He'd work off some steam, assuming the damn electrician had made progress.

Deacon expected to fly solo, but Noah was starting on the sprinkler system. He ambled over, but Noah didn't look up, "You're up early."

Deacon crouched beside him. "Couldn't sleep. What about you?"

The crinkle at the corner of Noah's eye gave away his smile. "I like getting ahead of the game." He rocked back on his heels. "And I like quiet."

Deacon agreed. "How's the electrical?"

Wordlessly, Noah glanced toward the van pulling up. "He's finishing up. The inspector's back tomorrow. You lit a fire under his ass."

Deacon scowled. Noah wanted answers. Deacon scrubbed his face with one hand. "I promised myself no more girl problems, ever. No girls, no problems. Introduce me to one, suddenly everything's a fucking problem."

Noah gawked. "This realtor has you all tied up in knots. Can't blame you. She's hot."

Deacon growled, running his fingers through his hair. He straightened, Noah standing next to him. "I was dealing with it. By that, I mean I ignored it."

"So, you need to get laid."

Deacon didn't answer. "I'm fucking human. She kissed me, sent my libido into overdrive. I didn't sleep with her," he added quickly. "But the idea kept me awake."

"Just do it," Noah chuckled.

"Not gonna happen," Deacon refused. "I'll work it off. You, on the other hand, could have given yourself a heart attack."

Noah looked sheepish. "Man, sometimes the pressure gets to me. The responsibility…" He trailed off and sighed. "It's hard to stay on track."

"People count on you. That's heavy. If you lose it, we all lose, and we could lose everything." Noah started to protest, but Deacon held up a hand. "I wouldn't have thrown a punch. You almost brawled."

Reluctantly, Noah said, "I'll work on it. But hear me, Deacon. Not all women are evil. Don't judge the tree by the rotten fruit."

"I hear you." But he didn't want to stick his toe in to test the water, just to have it bitten off by a piranha. "I'll be inside if you need anything." He clapped Noah on the back and ended the conversation.

All his brothers had been wronged. It's how they'd come together. But no one understood how betrayal had shattered him. The pieces of his heart never fit right again. He didn't know if he'd ever risk falling in love again.

At noon, an exhausted Deacon realized he hadn't eaten breakfast. He felt calmer and needed to apologize to Shiloh for being a dick. Sweat, dirt, and grime be damned, it was now or never and rode toward Shiloh's office in Mount Pleasant.

He parked in front of the door, considering Noah's words. Shiloh was obviously interested. But he needed to weigh the ramifications of exploring that.

Clenching his jaw at the pristine exterior of the building, Deacon chastised himself for not showering. He stunk of metal and heat. Shiloh would probably throw him out the second she took a breath.

The door dinged, announcing his arrival. Shiloh stood in the atrium, speaking to some guy in a pressed shirt, Chinos, and a loosened tie. His clean cut and carriage screamed money. Deacon hated him on principle. Shiloh cut a glance over but stood intimately close to him. She spoke too low to make out words, but her laugh rang loud as she touched the guy's arm flirtatiously.

Red rage coiled inside his chest. Like all women, Shiloh teased the dangerous type but gravitated to reputable, established men. She'd kissed him less than 24 hours ago in the heat of the moment. In the light of day, Deacon didn't have a bank roll or stability.

He'd never be 'the one'.

The man nodded politely as he passed by. "I didn't know you were coming." Shiloh stood too close, and his lack of awareness fueled his anger.

"I shouldn't have come," he muttered.

"I was going to call you." Her tone was bright, as if she hadn't practically thrown herself at the man who just left. Like she had at Deacon last night.

"Good," he replied shortly. "Call me." He started to leave.

She touched his arm. "What's wrong, Deacon?

He jerked away. "Save the charm for someone else." He took off, not looking back. He revved his engine and tore down the road without a destination. Far. That was his only thought.

Chapter 6

Deacon's defenses went up fast. He'd misread the interaction between Shiloh and Roger. Shiloh bolted into action. He'd left from fear, not disinterest.

Shiloh grabbed her purse and ran out as he buzzed down the road. She had to catch up and explain, crack that tough façade.

It took all her concentration to keep up. He drove like a maniac, and she weaved, switching from street racing to demolition derby.

She gasped as he nearly laid the bike down, taking a sharp curve too fast. Still, he rode on, and she followed. She cursed the red light that stopped her, relieved as Deacon pulled into a convenience store. This was her chance.

She tapped the steering wheel, antsy, and burned rubber when it turned green. Inside, she heard voices in a heated discussion, growing louder by the minute. She followed them, recognizing Deacon's timbre.

"Maybe you shouldn't eat all that shit, fat ass. Greasy fingers can't hold a drink!" Deacon poked a finger into some guy's chest in the back of the store.

"You're the piece of shit who ran in here and didn't watch your step!" the other guy threw back. Deacon's fists balled at his sides. Shiloh stepped in before she could talk herself out of it.

Ignoring Deacon's horrified expression, she beamed at the other guy, reaching into her purse. "We're sorry for the inconvenience. Here, take this." She handed him a ten and a business card. "For restitution. Come on, Deacon, we're leaving."

She could feel his breath on her neck, unmoving. She turned, putting both hands on his chest and shoving. "Go!" Glaring at her with, he stomped to the bike. Outside, Deacon grabbed her arm. Teeth clenched, he hissed, "What the fuck was that? I was handling it."

Shiloh scoffed. "Yeah, and looking at time for assault. I saved your ass. We need to talk. Follow me." She slammed into her car and drove. Behind her, he reluctantly threw a leg over the bike. She could have gone back to the office, but her house was closer.

31

She jerked into her driveway, Deacon squealing in behind, storming toward her. Shiloh refused to make a scene. She fumbled with the keys and nearly ripped the door off the hinges. She whirled as he stepped inside, fury clouding his eyes. "What do you want from me?" he demanded.

"To not get half-cocked because you're paranoid!" she tossed at him. Her chest heaved with boiling rage. "What was that about?"

He shook his head. "It doesn't matter. You shouldn't have stepped in."

Shiloh huffed. "Maybe you shouldn't have stormed out."

He laughed without humor. "You were all over that guy. I know women fantasize about the wild life, but you could have warned me before kissing me and going back to your rich bitch boy toy."

She gaped at him, hurt. "Is that what you think of me?"

He spread his hands. "I call it like I see it."

She spoke through clenched teeth. "Roger is a colleague, and he's gay. We went to school together. He helped me get my real estate license. I was clearing my debt. You could have asked, but you're too pigheaded to accept that I'm not your ex."

Some of the anger bled from his expression, replaced by shame. Good. He'd judged unfairly. "Why did you follow me?"

Shiloh squared her shoulders. "Like it or not, I care about you. And my reputation. I'm not some slut hitting on every swinging dick in town."

Deacon scowled. "You barely know me," he grunted.

"I know enough!" she cried out. She bit her lip. Now, Deacon would shut down, confronted by emotional investment.

She opened her mouth to apologize, but he swallowed her words, taking one long stride and covering her lips. The kiss was harsh, angry. She shoved her hands into his hair, feeding off the raw passion.

He yanked her roughly forward, pressed against him. The air sparked and his cock hardened. Her belly fluttered; her skin burned. The heat coiled between her legs, molten desire.

She gasped for air, Deacon's heart thudding against her shoulder. He locked eyes, his wild as if torn between jumping off a cliff without a parachute or running back down the mountain. She couldn't let him think too long.

She took his lips, molding to him. His cock twitched against her, stiffening to full mast. It had been too long. Shiloh wanted Deacon too much.

He walked her backward toward the couch. They tumbled onto the cushions, his weight bearing down on her. His muscles clenched as he moved against her.

Shiloh reached for the hem of his shirt, shoved her hands under, threading her fingers through the hair on his chest.

With deft fingers, he drew a line down her side and cupped her breast. Her skin ignited. She curled one leg around him, and he sank between her thighs. She cried out, his shaft pressing against her hot core.

He licked her jaw, suckled at her neck. Her nails bit into his body. He sat up and tore his shirt off. She wriggled from hers. His lips on the curve of her breast had her arching her back for more.

Heat poured from him, and her skin flushed, the warmth rushing through her until the moisture escaped between her thighs.

The air crackled as he spoke in a gruff voice, "Not here."

Shiloh panicked. Was he backing out? But he grabbed her hand and pulled her to her feet. She couldn't take her eyes off him as he sought out the bedroom.

Inside, he dropped her hand and threw her to the bed. In a whirlwind of motion, clothes flew. She drank in the sight of his thick, muscled legs and deeply toned chest.

He crawled over her, his fingers slicking in the wetness dripping from her. Shiloh closed her eyes and shivered. She whimpered as the head of his erection pushed at her opening.

Shiloh locked her legs around Deacon. He drove deep into her, then deeper with each forward motion of his hips, until they rocked together. He froze, shivering, the lack of control evident on his face.

In a strained voice, he croaked, "You feel so good. It's been so long."

The words nearly pushed Shiloh over the edge. "Take your time," she sighed.

And he did. He rolled his hips, and she met his thrusts, matching his slow pace. Deacon picked up speed, movements growing frantic. Shiloh saw the fireworks seconds before her body exploded. She screamed in ecstasy, clawing and writhing.

With a sharp gasp, Deacon shook with his release, immense pleasure on his face. He dropped onto her, heaving for air, and she etched the moment into her memory for safekeeping.

Euphoria enveloped her. She wouldn't break the spell.

Not yet.

Chapter 7

Deacon couldn't move. His heart pounded, bruising his chest. He needed to dress and get out. He'd thought satisfying the physical craving would curb his desire. Instead, he wanted to spend the rest of the day in bed with Shiloh.

What a fucking moron.

Shiloh was a business associate. Business and pleasure mixed about as well as oil and water. Besides, he couldn't trust her, couldn't risk betrayal. He rolled away and stared in surprise as she stood and collected her clothes.

She smiled, raking her eyes over him. "I left in such a hurry I didn't lock the door to the office. I have to get back."

His choices gave him little experience, but he hadn't expected aloofness. He reached for his jeans. "I get it." Had he failed to please her? Impossible. His body tensed as he recalled her walls quaking. Jesus, self-doubt? This woman had burrowed under his skin as he burrowed into her sweet, hot…

Fuck! She would be the death of him. "We need to talk business later," Shiloh said. "How about dinner? I'll cook."

He stilled. Here, he'd likely give into his desire. He might be a glutton for punishment but wouldn't go down that rabbit hole. They had to talk business, but he needed control.

He countered, "Let's meet somewhere."

A fleeting expression passed too quickly to discern. "Sure. Text me a time and place."

She combed her fingers through her hair. Deacon allowed himself one long look. Regret washed through his veins like a drug. He'd gotten a taste and wanted to drag her back to bed and start all over again.

What the fuck was he going to do?

She wrapped her arms around his waist and pushed up on her toes to kiss him gently. A far cry from her emotionless attitude moments ago.

It would be easier if she gave him the cold shoulder.

"That was amazing," she said, voice husky. "Please don't shut me out." She pulled away, and Deacon felt the weight of her words. He left in silence, battling himself. He'd lost everything last time he'd gotten tangled up with a woman. But a part of him long buried wanted to try again. Deep in his soul, he needed connection, and Shiloh stood out, different. The kind of woman he might fall for. He might trust.

If he was willing to fall again.

Out of the question! His trauma took on a personality, screaming inside. Just considering a relationship was alarming.

He straddled his bike and heaved a sigh. He needed advice, and he mourned he couldn't call his father. His club brothers would encourage him, whether to let go of his fears or to simply take advantage of Shiloh. He didn't want to hear either. His emotions, shut down for so long, roiled inside. His analytical father would have helped him rationalize the situation.

He didn't know when his parents drank the Kool-Aid, but it killed their relationship with Deacon. And it blindsided him, defied explanation. He couldn't consult the only man who might help.

And damn it, he still had to meet Shiloh for dinner!

With a growl, he made a one-eighty in the driveway, speeding off. Riddled with doubt, he needed an outlet. Right now, physical exertion would make his body stop twitching with the memory of Shiloh's touch. He'd go mad without the distraction. The sensation was too raw to ignore.

He reveled in the power of the bike beneath him. He'd always enjoyed riding, but he'd grown to love this beast. He understood the draw, the adrenaline rush, and the freedom of riding.

Maneuvering winding roads on the scenic route, Deacon forced himself to relax and meld with the bike. By the time he arrived, his spirits had lifted. He spotted Noah washing up. As Deacon neared him, Noah scowled. "Back for more?"

Deacon grinned. "I can't punish my body enough. What's the word?"

Toweling off, Noah gestured toward the electrician's van. "They're almost done. River tore down the fence. He's digging holes for posts. The new fence is priority. It'll hide the eyesore of the backyard and cut some construction noise."

"You got it." He strode past Noah, headed toward River, standing on a shovel on the far side of the backyard.

Deacon surveyed the progress. River had finished most of the digging. "You've been busy," he commented.

Throwing dirt from the hole, River wiped his brow, leaving a brown streak. He lifted his shirt and swiped again, mumbling in frustration. "The worst is done. You want to mix concrete? We finish the posts today, they'll be set enough to erect the fence tomorrow."

"Sounds like a plan."

***

Time ceased to matter as Deacon and River planted steel posts for an eight-foot fence They joked and chatted, sometimes falling silent, methodically filling holes with concrete around the poles before moving to the next spot.

"Shit," Deacon muttered, reaching for his phone and stopping himself just before globbing cement all over it.

"What's up?" River asked, straightening the post and stretching his back.

"I forgot something," he muttered, cleaning one hand enough to send a text. He'd completely forgotten to message Shiloh about dinner. He asked to swing by the project and sent the address.

When she didn't reply, Deacon cursed and tucked the phone away. One fuck-up after another. Doubt taunted him. Was she busy or ignoring him? Damn, he was neurotic over this shit.

He'd clear everything up tonight or tomorrow if necessary. He had to maintain the business relationship, for his brothers. For now, they had half the yard to finish. Clapping his hands, he told River, "We're burning daylight. Let's do this."

Chapter 8

Trying to curb her disappointment when she didn't hear from Deacon, Shiloh relented and agreed to show another client a house in Dangerfield.

His text came through as she arrived. It was an hour to Paris, and he was cancelling dinner. Shiloh had remained casual, but she'd asked him not to shut down. That probably sounded every alarm in Deacon's brain. Shiloh hated women like his ex.

She should have told Deacon she was moving on, but she wanted his money. Selfish and conniving. And that best friend? What an asshole. Shiloh might miss out on something brilliant, and it angered her. She struggled with pleasantries, rushing through the showing and anxious to leave.

Gritting her teeth, she shot a message to Deacon that she was on her way.

The drive gave her time to get nervous. She doubted he'd be alone. The tension between them would be palpable. No one could ignore it.

The daylight waned as she finally reached the project. She stared, wondering if she'd stepped into a Vegas fantasy. This looked like some sort of male revue on the strip.

Men littered the property in various states of disarray. Most were shirtless, glistening with sweat, muscles rippling, dirt or paint smeared on their hard bodies. Motorcycles parked three-deep for several yards looked like props for the show. She was shocked women weren't lined up with cameras.

She shook it off, intrigued at her lack of interest in all but one. And he might take offense to her casual observations.

She scanned for Deacon. "Can I help you?" The young man approaching her had just finished hanging shutters.

"I'm looking for Deacon." She trained her eyes on his face. Seriously, this would tempt a saint.

He smiled, showing perfect white teeth. "Backyard."

She thanked him and strode doggedly on, eyes fixed forward. She rounded the house, recognizing River from the club's first inquiry. Her heart flipped as Deacon straightened from a crouch next to him.

He looked primal, strong, arms caked in concrete and hair wet. He crouched again as she stepped up, and he looked at her, surprised. "I wasn't sure you were coming."

With a teasing grin, she told him, "I texted, but I see why you wouldn't get it." She glanced at River, who looked like he'd taken a mud bath. "Nice to see you."

"Yes, ma'am," he winked. "Likewise."

She glanced warily at the house. "I'm not sure where you expect to go over paperwork. And you're busy rolling in the dirt."

He stood and stretched, the sinewy muscles begging her to lick the deep cut lines. "We're finishing up. I need a shower. I'm offensive." He glanced at River, sharing some unspoken agreement as River walked away.

Shiloh heard excuses and felt rejected. She wasn't giving up, though. "You could wash, and we can sit in my car."

Deacon snorted. "You'd never get the grime out. I have a better idea," he said, surprising her. "I'll shower and order food. Meet me at home in an hour."

That was a wicked turn. She almost asked if this was, in fact, a date. But she bit her tongue. "Send me the address."

"Do you prefer Chinese or Mexican?"

Unable to resist, she let her eyes roam over him and quipped, "American." His eyes heated with warning. She shivered. "Either. I'm hungry." She winked.

He stepped close enough to catch his scent beneath the grime. She swallowed a moan. Deacon spoke so low she barely heard him. "Listen, if I overstepped my bounds—"

She stopped him with a hand on his chest and instantly regretted it. Those muscles were pumped to stone and slick, enticing. She pulled away and clinched her fist. "Please, save it."

He inhaled deeply. "I don't want anything ruining the business relationship for the sake of the club."

She spoke clearly, with emphasis. "I'm a professional. The only thing you could ruin is a chance at something incredible." With a teasing smile, she asked, "So, is tonight a date?"

She saw him battle indecision. "A casual one."

"Fair enough," she replied. "I'll see you in an hour."

"Yes, ma'am." His playful smile warmed her, and she forced her eyes away. She could watch him for days. She felt his eyes on her until she rounded the house out of his sight. As she gathered herself, River caught her attention.

"Got a minute?" His expression was troubled.

She only needed to change clothes. "Sure." He walked beside her.

"Deacon's got a thing for you." His eyes twinkled.

She swallowed a giggle. "You think so? He seems not to trust women."

River shrugged. "He's cautious. But he can't take his eyes off you." He grew serious. "I've never seen him like this, so if you're interested, a word to the wise."

"You have my attention," she said, curious.

"Be gentle. And patient. He got shafted pretty bad. But he'll pull his head out of his ass." River had his friend's interest at heart, and Shiloh appreciated the information.

"So, I'm not spinning my wheels," she teased.

47

"Not if you're the right woman." He winked at her.

Shiloh nodded. "I'll keep it in mind." Deacon thought love was a lost cause, but not everyone thought he was. And clearly, his brothers saw his interest. Hopefully, they'd be discrete, as River had, and not scare him.

At home, Shiloh donned a flirty dress and checked her messages, relieved to see the address. Excitement crept through her like a vine. Tonight could be a turning point.

Sleeping with Deacon fed her emotions, and they'd bloomed like a mushroom cloud. Deacon thought of himself as broken. Hopefully, he'd take one more chance. She gathered her purse and slipped on sandals. Her phone chimed, but she refused to look. If Deacon got cold feet, she wanted plausible deniability.

Face to face, he wouldn't turn her away.

When she arrived, Shiloh knocked, and Deacon answered. He was freshly showered, skin glowing and hair slicked back. He wore jeans that showed every leg muscle with a ribbed tank exposing enough to remind her what lay beneath.

With a devastating grin, he pushed the door wider. She sidled past him, brushing against him with an electrical spark. Yeah, she was putty in his hands. Casual date, he said. And business to tend. She could be patient…for a while.

Chapter 9

Deacon kicked himself. The dress clung to the curve of her breasts. He should've never changed the plans. He could have showered and met her somewhere.

He could rationalize outside her presence. Out of sight, out of mind. But he had opened the door, and his resolve and self-control had flushed down the toilet like a load of shit.

Business first. The Suns had expectations. He could fulfill obligations before he fucked up his entire personal life, right?

"Welcome," he greeted. "I ordered tacos. I had a craving."

"Tacos. My weakness." She took in the surroundings. Deacon didn't have a lot of décor. An army blanket draped on the couch, a few old photos of friends, a world map.

"I see you got cleaned up," she remarked, perching on the edge of the love seat.

"I reeked of sweat," he chuckled. He sat across from her. "You spiffed up. I like the dress."

"Thanks," she said, averting her gaze. She didn't take compliments well.

Silence invited action, and that was dangerous, so he sought conversation. "You want something to drink? I've got beer, soda, and water."

"I could use a water. Thanks."

Returning with a bottle, he hedged, "I'm too anxious to wait. Do we have an offer?"

She handed him some paperwork. "We've got several, but I brought the three best. I say accept the second-highest. It's cash and will clear escrow in two weeks. That gives you a higher profit margin."

He quirked a brow. "How much is it?"

She grinned broadly. "Fifteen grand over asking price. A quick turnaround also gives you working capital faster. You can invest some in a high yield account, too, and let the money grow." She pointed to the figures. "It's a lot of information, but that's the number."

This was huge. They'd expected to wait weeks or even months. People liked their product, and it filled Deacon with pride. "I'm overriding the need for approval. We'll accept before they change their minds. Thank you, Shiloh. You put our work in the right light."

"You did it," she pointed out. "I just showed it. Congrats. I'll let them know you accept." She pulled out her phone and started texting madly.

Nervous energy had him pacing. "You think it'll go this well next time?"

"Quality work and a good cause? People will clamor for it," she laughed. "Although, I noticed some serious safety hazards at the jobsite."

He scowled at her. "Like?"

She snorted. "Shirtless men, no safety goggles or hardhats. No gloves. No protective covering. I didn't know construction was done half naked."

Her eyes roamed his chest. It spurred his ego. He gave a cocky grin. "We're not union. This is how good southern boys work, sweetheart."

Shiloh rolled her eyes. "Please! My roots are deeper south than this. Laredo, remember?"

"And you came here to escape what?"

She hesitated, piquing his curiosity. Would she share her past freely like he had?

"I escaped failure. After high school, options are limited. I'm not a career store clerk. I ran with the MCs. They're bad news. You can marry a roughneck, have kids, never see your husband. Or you can leave."

Deacon scowled. "So you left."

"Not soon enough." She averted her gaze. "I got involved with a biker. It's not a 'thing' for me," she rushed, looking him square in the eye. "I was young, bored. His life seemed exciting. I left to better myself, to escape that life."

Deacon silently cursed the timing of the doorbell. He grabbed the food and hurried back to continue the conversation. "Why real estate?"

"Roger. He thought it would fit my personality and paid for courses. When I got my license, the Dallas market was ripe, but I wanted to land somewhere that wasn't on most maps. This is the place. For now."

Why would she want to hide? He held his tongue, trying to show trust. Whatever secrets she had would come out in time. If he could quell his fears.

As they ate, she hedged, "Your club is so different from the crowd I grew up with. I questioned whether I could trust y'all. I wish more clubs were so clean and honest."

He grunted. "I had concerns. Most clubs run drugs or weapons, or they're hired muscle. But the Suns work for others first. I needed that, and the family." Even with the club, he'd barely escaped the darkness of PTSD and grief.

He admired Shiloh. She had a fire inside glowing bright, drawing him in. It gave her spirit, drive. She took care of herself. Tara never had. Unlike Shiloh, she was an opportunist.

As they cleaned up, her phone sounded, and they froze. Deacon waited as she checked the message, hoping it was confirmation of the sale. But her expression soured, her skin bleak, and she dropped to the couch. What the hell?

Chapter 10

Why now? Shiloh swallowed her fear, refusing to answer the taunting message. She closed her phone and slipped it into her purse. Deacon watched her with concern. "Don't tell me that was nothing," he said, his voice tight.

How much should she tell him? Biting her lip, Shiloh knew honesty meant everything. His trust had been broken, and she had to walk a fine line. The truth might send him packing, but holding back definitely would. She'd never win him with lies and half-truths. She took a deep, shuddering breath.

"My ex." The words caught in her throat. She reached for the water, parched. Funny how old ghosts could haunt you.

Deacon tensed. "What did he do to you, Shiloh? Why are you hiding from him?" Bloodlust had his eyes dark, dangerous.

Shiloh shook her head. "It's not what he did, it's who he is." She didn't miss his decision to sit beside her. As if she needed the comfort and support to help her through this. She was grateful.

"Cody ran deep with the gangs. He got into illegal shit early on. He stole things, sold them for profit. He used drugs on and off, pushed them, ran them. Border towns have easy access to a lot, and he was never the cautious guy. Rarely thought things through. And when he used, he was a mean son of a bitch. He had a horrible temper. He cheated, picked fights. I saw him hurt other women."

"Did he hurt you?" Deacon spoke through clenched teeth, with barely contained rage, and she heard the inherent need to protect her. It felt good. She'd never experienced that before.

She shrugged. "He didn't get very physical with me. He might grab my wrist too tight and force me to follow him. He was verbally abusive toward the end. I literally watched the violence escalate. I was scared to leave. He had eyes and ears everywhere. But I left before he hurt me." Finally meeting his gaze, she said, "I called Roger. He was the only person I trusted, and I knew he'd gotten out of the area. The rest you know. I enrolled in real estate classes and started my business with a couple of dimes, a hope, and a prayer."

Something sparked in Deacon's eyes. Jealousy? No, thankfully not. Understanding. "Remind me to thank him for taking care of you. Helping you the one time you couldn't help yourself."

That shocked her, but her heart leapt. Roger was important to her. And inadvertently, Deacon had just admitted to caring about her wellbeing. Catching feelings, she hoped. "I've changed my number, worked with mostly cash instead of cards, sent mail to my mother under a different name at a PO Box. His gang has a long reach, but Roger's helped me there, too. But it's obviously not enough. Cody has my number."

"If he's threatening you—"

Shiloh held up a hand. "It's not that simple. He's a stalker at heart. He'll hound me until I come out of hiding, tired of the mind games. It's psychological warfare."

"What did he say?" Deacon demanded.

Shiloh hesitated. "Does it matter?"

Deacon stiffened. "You do business with the club. We protect our interests." Shiloh's hopes fell, but he spoke lower, fiercer. "I protect *my* interests." With a shaking hand, he reached and tucked a strand of hair behind her ear. She shivered, accepting his gentle, reassuring kiss. "It matters."

Her shoulders slumped. She let herself accept his support, knowing how difficult it was for him to offer freely. "He says if I don't meet him to talk, he'll burn my business to the ground. Then my house."

"He'll never get past the club," Deacon clipped, punching his lap. "We'll have security posted round the clock, on you, your house, and the office."

Shiloh couldn't ask that. They had important work to do, and that work provided all their paychecks, as well as resources for homeless vets. "You have deadlines to meet. I can't take your resources."

"You *are* our resource, Shiloh. I'll be damned if I'm going to put my heart out there for you and not keep you safe." He clammed up, his eyes wide, but her heart turned a flip as their eyes locked. He took a deep breath. "I don't know how to do this, but I want to try. You make me want to put the pieces of my heart back together and try."

The words wrapped her in a soft blanket of elation. "I'd like that," she said quietly. She'd already fallen hard. But what about Cody? He knew where to find her, and that had to be resolved before she could move forward with Deacon. Cody would come after Deacon. He specialty was leveraging what meant the most against you. It's why she'd feared leaving him.

"Let's get rid of this piece of shit for good. He may have loyalty through fear, but he's got nothing on us. Loyal brothers, military men, trained in combat, and all with wounded souls." He scowled. "I need to make some calls. Are you okay?"

"Yes. Thank you, Deacon."

He looked torn but reached for her, pulling her into a tight embrace and kissing her with promise. "Let me handle business so we can move on to pleasure."

***

Deacon had men on Shiloh's home and office within an hour. One good thing about small towns, nothing was far away. They'd iron out details later. He had no intention of letting Shiloh leave tonight. He'd keep her safe here, in his arms.

His protective instinct hit like a gale force wind, all the emotions he'd tried to hide flooding him. Shiloh continued to prove him wrong, and he'd let his guard down too far and too long. She'd climbed over the fence and planted herself within his walls.

And damn, he wanted to keep her there, whatever the cost.

Her vulnerability made his chest ache. She'd left trouble behind, launched a successful career, a natural in real estate. And still the past came to haunt her. Just as his past had recently reared its ugly head. Fate? Destiny? Maybe the reminder allowed him to see the vast difference, open to new possibilities.

Deacon's desire didn't fade. It morphed into something more. A need to help, protect, and cherish as strong as the yearning to worship her body. He wanted to tear her clothes off, but bringing her a blanket and fresh brewed hot tea was more fulfilling. It felt right, and her presence took away a chill he hadn't noticed. Now, it was cozy, welcoming, like the house that already had an offer.

"He won't go away," she said quietly leaning back. Deacon draped an arm casually behind her. "He'll keep coming. He'll stalk me until he finds something I care about enough that he can use it against me."

Deacon had planned attacks before, with other strategists. He'd known his team, and they'd known the enemy. Now, he had Shiloh, who knew the enemy, and he knew his brothers. "Let him bait you," he said slowly, working through it. "Just for a day or two. Ignore the texts. Then, agree to meet him."

Shiloh stared at him, jaw slack. "And then what?"

Deacon gave a sinister grin. "Then, we ambush."

"You can't start trouble, Deacon. You can't risk your freedom, or your life." She wrung her hands.

He toyed with her hair. "No fighting. But we'll put the fear of god in him. And the rest of his crew." She looked skeptical, and he sighed. "I'll work with the cops, if necessary. Stalking and threats are illegal. Sheriff Burton will shit his pants at the opportunity to cage a biker." He laughed. "Trust me, okay?"

Her expression eased, the tension fading. "I do. I've trusted you from the day I met you."

Sheepishly, he replied, "I wish I could say the same. Damaged goods, Shiloh. Don't make excuses for me or walk on eggshells. But remember I've locked myself away for nearly ten years. And I can be a slow learner."

"Yeah?" She twisted to face him, tucking her legs under her. "You seem to learn your way around a woman's body pretty quickly, for someone with so little experience."

Deacon inhaled sharply. Her pupils widened, and his groin tugged. "I'm detail oriented. I watch and take in feedback." He remembered now her expression when she came. Her breasts swayed, her breathing labored. Tension filled the air, the chemistry too strong, and he lost his resolve.

He leaned in to take her mouth, and she returned the kiss savagely.

Chapter 11

Shiloh knew the difference between comfort and craving. This wasn't sex to sooth her soul or chase away her fear. It wasn't a distraction. The emotions ran as strong between them as the physical need as he laid her back and rained kisses down her body. This was unadulterated longing.

She wouldn't call it love. Not yet But it was the foundation. She moaned as he pushed her skirt up and licked her inner thigh, nibbling softly. It was her sweet spot, made her drip, and it drove her mad as he sniffed the moisture. His groan vibrated through her, and she writhed, reaching to pull him up.

She felt animalistic and ripped his shirt from his chest. He chuckled with a deep rasp. "I have dozens. That was hot."

She smiled as he removed her dress, his eyes dancing at the sight of her bare breasts. He molded them, teased her already swollen nipples, and kissed her deeply. He rested his cock enticingly against her core. Her train of thought derailed, acting on instinct and releasing his erection from the tight jeans. He kicked them away. "The bedroom—"

Shiloh shook her head. "No, I want you here. Now."

His eyes rolled back in his head, and she reveled in his reaction. She couldn't resist him and wanted him to feel the same. He buried his face in her neck, biting and kissing, thrusting in with one long stroke. Sparks flew, and starbursts blinded her with the release.

She clawed at him, wanting more, and he moved in a smooth, determined rhythm, building friction and heat as her moisture lubricated his strokes. She held tight, almost melding into him. Their skin bonded, their bodies colliding. When he stuttered and clenched his jaw, Shiloh came again. He cried out, spilling hot and heavy as she shook with the force of the shared orgasm.

Peeling apart was a fruitless effort. Her limbs fell too heavy. His weight on her was welcome. Their labored breathing slowed together, until their hearts calmed, syncing together. She could have slept like this.

Eventually, as the euphoria faded into lazy satisfaction, Deacon stood, half carrying her to bed

64

and tucking her in. Inviting her to stay? In his bed? That was progress, she thought as she dozed off.

***

Shiloh couldn't find a phone charger and had to make sure her phone had enough battery for client calls. She had one in the car. Darkness still coated the window outside. She reached for a t-shirt lying over a chair, pulling it on. It covered enough. And if Deacon's neighbors were out at this hour, they'd get a peep show.

Grabbing the keys from her purse, she quietly let herself out and opened her car door, reaching for her cord. She gasped as an arm circled her waist and pulled her back. "Look what I found, a half-naked woman."

Shiloh seized at the familiar voice. She didn't fight, could tell from his breath he'd been drinking. Who knew what else he was on? "And who did you drop your panties for?" Cody asked, shoving her into the driver's seat. He crouched in front of her, blocking her escape. She couldn't crawl across the seat without him grabbing her.

"What do you want?" she asked. His eyes were wild, and he carried a pistol, tucked by his side. She cursed herself for not carrying protection.

"I thought I made it clear," he said, his hand snaking up her thigh. She bit her lip and didn't flinch. It might trigger violence. "I want you. It's all I've ever wanted. But here you are, spreading your legs for some random dick who'll just throw you away tomorrow like the worthless piece of shit you always were."

Shiloh pushed her hands into her lap, hoping to block his advance. "We can talk if you want, though I don't know why you want me if I'm worthless. But can we go somewhere else so I can put some clothes on? I'm cold." Any excuse to get his hands off her.

He smirked. "Are you inviting me over? I'll warm that ass right up." The smile faded. "I'm not sure I want sloppy seconds, though."

Good, she didn't want any part of Cody. "We should go. Before he wakes up." Shiloh glanced toward the house. She didn't want Deacon out here with Cody's gun to his head, or surrounded by other lowlifes. "My office is close, and I have some pants there."

He looked skeptical but nodded, pushing her. "Drive." He nearly slammed her leg in the door and crawled in the back. Her hands trembled as she turned the key, and she thought fast, hoping she could find an open gas station for help.

But most small towns didn't stay open twenty-four hours.

At her office, she had locking doors and multiple phones. She could put space between them, maybe long enough to dial 911.

Or speed dial 3. She had more faith in Deacon than the police.

As she drove, she tried to ignore Cody's constant muttering. He waved the gun absently, increasing her anxiety, rambling about nothing and then peppering loud insults for her into the rant. So hateful, and yet, so obsessed.

The office loomed ahead, dark and ominous in the night. Shiloh tried to stop shaking as she took the keys and unlocked it. She almost let the alarm sound, but the gun stopped her. She keyed the pin and gulped. "Can I please get dressed?" she asked politely.

He waved his hand, wrinkling his nose in disgust. "Whatever. I smell his stink on you. Filthy whore. Cover your shit up."

This was her chance. She stepped into her office, leaving the door open against suspicion. As she reached for her spare pants, she hit the speaker button, dialed '3', and muting the other end of the line, praying Deacon picked up. She jumped when Cody came around the corner, slamming his fist against the wall. "What's taking so long?"

"I'm dressed," she said, sitting in the desk chair. It put the desk between them. She glanced at the phone, saw the open line. It only slightly calmed her. "What do you want to talk about, Cody?" Deacon would recognize the number, hopefully the name.

Cody laughed, high pitched, pacing the room. "You left, Shiloh. Up and left and didn't say anything."

"I got a job," she said simply. "I tried to call. You were out of town."

He snarled, kicking the desk. "I came back. You should have been there."

"I had to jump on the opportunity. I had no future in Laredo." The line stayed lit. Deacon could be here in ten minutes, if she just kept Cody talking.

"I was your future!" he exploded, beating his chest with bruising force. "I had you covered. You didn't need a job. I make bank, Shi."

68

"Not legitimately." She kept her voice low and even. *Don't.* "I don't want those things, Cody. Cheating. Theft. Drugs. Lies. That's why we didn't work."

"Oh, we didn't?" He glared at her, sneering. "You think I'm done with you?" He shook his head. "I don't care how many other guys got inside you. You're mine. We're done when I say we're done."

Repulsed, she swallowed a gag. "My body belongs to me, no one else."

"Are you turning me down?" he asked, incredulous. "You'll fuck this random thug, and who knows how many others, but you tell me no? Get over yourself. I take what I want."

Damn. She'd tried to reason with him but just stirred the hornet's nest. He came across the desk, pinning her in the chair before she could move. Terror ran cold through her veins, and she feared Cody would get what he wanted before help arrived.

Chapter 12

Deacon didn't wait for his crew. He barked orders at Noah through the home phone, his cell to his ear as he raced.

He'd paced frantically when he woke to find Shiloh gone, her car missing. He panicked finding her phone by the bed. His rational mind fell prey to worst case scenarios. When her office number rang, he answered with a cry. "Shiloh!"

Shiloh's voice came through over background noise, but she didn't answer. *Cody*. The asshole ex. How the hell had he gotten her? She'd been tucked in next to Deacon. As he bolted to action, he guessed she'd gone to her car for something. His door was unlocked, and her purse was there but not the keys.

What was this guy capable of? Would he hurt Shiloh?

He revved the bike, pushing it to its limit. She'd gone to the office, not her house. Smart girl. But Deacon didn't know if her captor was alone or leading a crew, not from the audio he had. He'd called for backup. Safety in numbers.

"Put the gun down!" Shiloh screamed, the words piercing his eardrum through the earpiece. "Cody, no!"

Fear ripped through him, and Deacon screamed wordlessly, praying he wasn't too late. He squealed into the parking lot and dropped the bike. It could be fixed. The gunshot rang through the earpiece and cracked the air simultaneously. He dove for the entrance, but Reid shoved him aside. "I've got firepower, brother," he called as he ran past.

Deacon was steps behind, taking stock of the situation. Reid leveled his gun at a disheveled man on the floor, outside Shiloh's office. He looked stunned, blood soaking his jeans. The world stopped turning. Deacon didn't care about the piece of shit. He leapt over him, his eyes darting frantically around the office.

Shiloh crouched in the corner, shaking, eyes unfocused. A pistol lay in front of her. Other than some blood spatter, she seemed unharmed. Deacon drew her into his arms, and she clung to him like a child. "You're okay now," he assured her, tucking her face into his chest. He spoke soothingly. "I'm here. Did he hurt you?"

Sniffling, Shiloh shook her head. "He…he came at me with the gun, but he was too focused on…" She trailed off, shivering. Deacon didn't need her to say more. He might just tear the asshole limb from limb. "I wrestled the gun away. I just pointed and shot." She finally met his gaze. "You're here." It came out like a long sigh.

Deacon's jaw muscle twitched. "Of course I'm here. I'll always be here." It was a hard pill to swallow, but he knew it was true. He kissed her cheeks, her forehead, the tip of her nose. Then, he sat in the chair and pulled her into his lap.

Reid was unleashing expletives at Cody, maybe smacking him around. Noah leaned in, saying quietly, "The cops are here." He pulled the door closed, blocking some of the noise outside. Too bad, Deacon rather enjoyed Reid's creative insults. But Shiloh calmed and stopped shivering. "I shouldn't have gone outside," she whispered. "I needed a charger."

Deacon sighed. "Next time, wake me up," he growled, the pain of near loss excruciating. His attachment to Shiloh bloomed far too quickly, bigger and stronger than he'd ever had with Tara. After tonight, Deacon would stay the course. He didn't know if he could live without her.

"Next time?" she asked with a sad laugh. She sat up and reached for a tissue. "I wouldn't blame you if you ran from the drama."

He cupped her chin in one hand and forced her to gaze to his. "He's going to prison, for a long time. And we'll pick his crew apart. There's no more drama." He smiled, nervous excitement overriding fear. "And I'll deal with whatever drama comes around. I like a warm body beside me at night. And the idea of a bright smile in the morning."

She stared at him, obviously conflicted. "Deacon, I don't want to scare you away…"

He shook his head adamantly. "I'm not running away. I'm in love with you. It hit like a ton of bricks when I thought you were gone. You have my heart. And I trust you won't throw it away."

Shiloh gulped, a tear sliding down her cheek. "I can't promise not to hurt you, but I love you. And I'll try to keep your heart safe." She brushed her thumb over his lips. "We'll figure it out together."

He nodded. "Together." He touched her nose with the tip of his finger. "I'm ready, Shiloh." He knew those were larger words than 'love', and she beamed through her tears, through the fear still haunting her eyes. Yes, he trusted her, and he loved her. And he intended to spend a great deal of time getting used to it.

Because he still knew shit about women and fully expected Shiloh to teach him.

The bell on the door clinked just as Rylan hung up the phone, and she smiled before she even looked up at the man walking through the door, still making notes from the call. "Good morning. Welcome to Workplace Staffing. How can I help you today?" It was always a toss-up whether walk-ins wanted work or wanted workers.

"Good morning, ma'am. My name is Drew Evans, and I'm looking for a little short-term help on some projects."

The rich, deep voice caught her attention, and she glanced up through her lashes, blowing a few strands of tawny hair from her face. Her breath caught in her throat, and she struggled to maintain that smile, pasting it in place so she wouldn't show how flustered she was. Men of this caliber rarely walked through her door. He was an incredible specimen, with dark blue eyes, a chiseled face, and roguish long bleached hair. His smile came easy and had a teasing look.

She could have slid right into the floor, under her desk. "It's a pleasure, Mr. Evans. I'm Rylan Walsh, and I'd be happy to find you a few candidates to interview."

He scratched his head and then shoved his hands in the pockets of jeans that hugged his hips and emphasized just how toned he was. "See, that's the problem, ma'am. I don't really do interviews. I'm better at chitchat. And honestly, if I'm going to shoot the shit, I'd rather be speaking to a beautiful woman than some hairy construction worker."

Did he wink at her? Rylan swallowed hard. She motioned to the chair across the desk from her, watching the way his muscles rippled under his crisp white button down. He sat easily, slouching in the chair and rubbing his fingers along the thin line of hair over his lip. "Now, that's more like it. I get to speak to a beautiful woman. And please, call me Drew."

Her cheeks heating with the blush, Rylan looked down at her desk for a moment to collect herself. She probably came off as demure. Her thoughts were anything but.

Leah Rhoades lives in Texas and has been writing since childhood. Aside from being passionate about all things biker and paranormal, she enjoys spending time with her young son, Tristan, and watching horror movies.

www.ingramcontent.com/pod-product-compliance
Lightning Source LLC
Chambersburg PA
CBHW071949120726
48001CB00005B/2095